SONIC

THE HEDGEHOG

THE OFFICIAL MOVIE
NOVELIZATION

PENGUIN YOUNG READERS LICENSES
An Imprint of Penguin Random House LLC, New York

Visit us online at www.penguinrandomhouse.com.

ISBN 9780593093016   10 9 8 7 6 5 4 3

SONIC

THE HEDGEHOG

THE OFFICIAL MOVIE NOVELIZATION

*(That means it's a book version of everything
cool that happened in the movie.)*

by Kiel Phegley

CHAPTER 1

He had to go fast. Faster than a jet plane. Faster than the speed of sound. Faster than lightning. Sonic had to be the fastest thing alive.

What choice did he have with the missiles on his heels?

Crash! Shoooom!

"Hey, come on, Doc! You're trashing public property here!" Sonic called over his shoulder.

The shards of breaking glass fell in slow motion behind him. Sonic curved his path, and his whole body spun in a blue blur out onto San Francisco Bay. As he splashed out across the water, he could feel the first heat-seeker barreling down on him. And behind it he could hear the laughter of a certain maniac with bad breath and a weirdo mustache. Robotnik.

Even with the craziness of that egg-shaped pod of destruction close behind, Sonic couldn't stop asking himself how he got to this point. Where did this adventure all start? California? Planet Earth? These weren't places where a talking blue hedgehog was supposed to exist. Not like home.

Maybe that's where it all started. Back home. Back with Longclaw . . .

The island was as mysterious as it was

beautiful. Lush green plant life sprung from the ground in perfect geometric patterns. Crystal clear waterfalls cascaded into endless sandy beaches. And the ground twisted and turned not into hills but wild loops that only he could spring through without falling. And when he ran around them, there was music in the air.

But there was danger there, too. She had warned him.

Longclaw was the last of her kind, a noble line of warrior owls dedicated to maintaining balance for all living creatures. Outfitted in blades and battle armor, Longclaw's order had fought for years to protect their world—a world where the animals of the forest and the fields had evolved to be the dominant species; a world ruled by claw and fang.

But by the time Sonic knew her, the old

owl was less a radical warrior and more a wise mother. She was the only one who had cared for him after the emergence of his powers. Even in their world, the blue fur . . . the electric speed . . . it was nearly indescribable. There were some who believed his powers would unleash chaos on the world.

And so Longclaw took him into hiding on the island. There he could run free and be something close to a normal kid. The most chaotic things about his life were his hilarious pranks. That's how he saw it.

Whooooosh!

Wind whipped through the old hut they shared on that last night. Longclaw reached for the scabbard of her ancient blade. Her wings twitched as she called, "Who goes there?"

"Ha! Gotcha again!" Sonic laughed as he popped out from under the bed's covers. He'd just hit the place with an immense amount of wind.

"Sonic!" Longclaw called, leaning on her weapon for support. "You can't go bouncing across the island like that! Someone could have seen you."

"No one saw me—I'm too fast! And anyway, I wanted to bring you this."

He lifted up a sunflower, radiant and delicate. They grew on the far side of the island. The one that pointed back to the rest of the world.

The old owl took the blossom in her feathers and touched it gingerly. Then her eyes snapped into focus. She heard something. "Get down!" Longclaw shouted, and wrapped Sonic in her mighty wings.

Thunk! Thunk! Thunk!

A flash of arrows flew through the

windows and embedded themselves in the hut's weak walls.

A split second later, Longclaw blasted through the roof with Sonic clenched firmly in her talons. On the edges of his vision, Sonic could see who had fired the arrows: echidnas! They were coarse, vicious cousins of hedgehogs. And the hoods these ones wore showed their allegiance to the powerful warlords who had chased Sonic his whole life. They wanted to unleash the chaos energy inside him and overtake the world.

And by visiting the far side of the island where he'd most certainly been spotted, he'd led them right to his home.

The echidnas swarmed everywhere around the hut. Their army marched dark trails across the face of the beautiful island like black veins. There was no escaping them or the arrows that reached into the sky after Longclaw and Sonic.

Thwock!

"Arrrgggh!" Longclaw cried as her flapping ceased and both she and Sonic crashed to the forest floor. Sonic rose to his feet, but she stumbled again. The echidnas would be on them at any moment, but all he could think about was the wound he saw on Longclaw where the arrow bit deep into her side.

"Listen carefully, Sonic," she coughed as she limped to his side. "You have a power unlike anything I've ever seen. And that means someone will always want it. The only way to stay safe is to stay hidden. And you'll have to do it without me."

"NO!" Years later, Sonic still remembered the sting of tears in his eyes. "I'll shock them all until they never come for us again!"

"It's too late for that. And besides, you don't want to live only to destroy. You were meant for more than chaos," she said, like she had a thousand times before. "I don't know why this power came to you, but I have to believe that it was for more than being a pawn in someone else's game. That's why you must use the rings to travel to another planet—one whose inhabitants are ignorant of the larger universal order."

She showed him how they worked, the golden rings of almost unimaginable power. But Longclaw always warned Sonic that their powers were finite. He could hold one in his hands, imagine a place he wanted to travel, and the ring would expand to warp him where he wanted to go. But then it would dissipate. He didn't have many rings left, and he didn't dare put them to use unless it was absolutely necessary. This was the last thing she made him promise.

"Stay secret. Stay safe," Longclaw had said as a brutal coughing overtook her. "You can travel with one to this 'Earth' first. It may be easier to survive there. But if they ever find you, these humans will do terrible things to you, Sonic. I've seen what they're capable of. So if you're ever cornered, keep this place in your mind."

She lifted a ring and called forth an image of a faraway planet. Its luscious green valleys and streams were populated everywhere by massive mushrooms—bright shades of red and green and purple that were beautiful to look at but ultimately empty.

"What if I just spoke to a few of them? The humans?" Sonic had asked. "Someone I could trust!"

"Trust no one!" Longclaw said, gasping with her final breaths. "Promise me!"

"I . . . I promise," he said.

It had either been the smartest choice or the biggest mistake of his life, but the promise had been made.

No need to guilt-trip myself about it now, he thought as the missiles sped ever closer.

Because now that he was possibly facing his own end at the hands of Robotnik, Sonic finally understood what Longclaw had meant. This adventure with the humans was dangerous and deadly.

So where did this story really begin? It

was in Green Hills. Months ago. On the side of the road where Sonic finally connected with his only friend. And his only hope.

CHAPTER 2

Tom Wachowski hadn't expected nonstop action when he signed up for the force. *Maybe the occasional car chase,* he thought, *or it'd be nice to foil a smuggling ring now and then.* He certainly hadn't thought serving as a police officer in Green Hills meant shoot-outs and explosions all day long.

But as he sat in his squad car at the town's only speed trap where no one ever seemed to speed by, it was as if Tom could feel all the excitement in the world passing him by.

Deet-deet!

Tom's radar gun flickered to life and registered a pathetic "1.0 mph" on its screen.

"Excuse me, sir, but where's the fire?" he called out the window. "We got kids livin' around here!"

In the street ahead of him, a fat green turtle shrugged his way across the gravel, unimpressed.

"Sorry," Tom said in mock distress. "I thought that was kinda funny myself."

That was how Tom's days went in Green Hills. In the morning, clock turtles here on Route 9. Before lunch, save a cat out of Mrs. Porter's tree. Then spend the night shift getting soaked pushing Farmer Zimmer's pickup out of the mud. Everything just crawled on by.

Green Hills was home. It always had been. And Tom knew every picket fence, public park, and lemonade stand in it. The town had all kinds of people living in its limits, and Tom's job was to treat them all with the same respect. Just like his dad had done before him. It was the Wachowski family calling. But it wasn't enough.

"Sergeant Sprinkles," Tom said, leveling his eyes at the plastic donut cartoon character that sat on his dash. "If your investigation turns up anything happening in Green Hills—anything at all—please forward it to me immediately so I don't totally lose my mind from boredom."

The plastic figure sat inert.

"Best cop on the force," said Tom.

Deet-deet!

The red numbers on Tom's radar gun lit

up. He straightened in his seat and checked the screen. "Two hundred and eighty-three miles per hour?" Tom asked while checking his rearview mirror to see all of zero jet planes speeding down the road. "Thing must be broken."

Deet-deet!

The radar went off again in his hands. This time it read 296 mph. Tom gripped his steering wheel as if a tornado might pick him up off the ground. He waited. But nothing happened.

Suddenly, a shadow zipped across his rearview mirror. But it wasn't on the road. Something was lurking on the shoulder, some prankster out to play with Tom's relaxing afternoon.

Tom spun around like a gunslinger in the Old West and pointed his radar right where

he thought he saw the shadow. *Deet-deet!*
299 mph. Things were getting freaky now.

"I better check this out, Sarge," Tom said as
he opened the cruiser door and stepped out.
"Cover my six, partner."

In a flash, a swirling dust cloud kicked up
around Tom.

Deet-deet! Deet-deet! Deet-deet! The radar
went crazy. 300 then 302 then 305 mph!

Then suddenly . . . *SCHWOOOOOOM!*
went the wind, blowing Tom back and onto
the gravel ground.

BLOORP! The radar gun went off in his
hand, but this time it didn't even register a
number. Too fast to even clock.

"Sarge, you better call this in," Tom said as
he stood up. But his plastic partner was more
absent than usual. Sergeant Sprinkles had
disappeared into thin air.

Tom crept around the cruiser. The gust of wind that had knocked him down had blown away from the road like the smoke trail of a rocket. An eerie calm hung over the scene as he stepped up the slope away from the road. Here and there, the grass was flattened down, making a trail up and into the woods.

With slow steps, Tom walked up the path until it stopped in the middle of the hillside. There was a circular divot there, like a launching pad. The ground was warm, and sitting in the middle of the flattened blades of grass was something glowing—something blue.

Tom picked it up slowly. It shimmered in his hand like something electrified, but it didn't hurt. It was a needle, about as long as Tom's forearm. Or was it, maybe, some kind of . . . quill?

"Well, it's official, Tom," he said to himself.

"You've caught the crazy. It's time to get the heck out of Green Hills before the condition becomes permanent."

The rest of Tom's day delivered the same mix of boring and oddly mysterious. He played crossing guard for the town's most beloved raft of ducks. And things were looking up when a code 674 (disorderly conduct at the local watering hole) came in over the radio. Maybe he'd get to do some real police work and not just play animal control.

But, of course, it was just Carl again.

"Don't laugh at me, man. I seen it. I seen it clearer than anybody ever has!" The old nut was harmless, really. But Carl upset people when he got too animated about his conspiracy theories. It didn't help that certain folks in town egged him on.

"So if you saw this thing, Carl, what exactly did it look like?" The bartender smirked as Tom walked up to the small circle of patrons.

"Of course you guys called me for story hour," Tom said. "Why would anyone in this town call the police because of actual danger?"

"Oh, Tom! Thank goodness you're here!" Carl leaped onto a chair to tell his tale with shaking hands. "That's just the thing about the phenomenon on the edge of Green Hills! It's a blur. Haunting houses in town and making mischief; disappearing pies and TP-ing your houses at night. He's a blue devil! I tells ya, he's here to terrorize this town!"

"I'm sure you saw something, Carl." Tom

led him outside while thinking of the quill that still sat in the back of his car. "I've got to hope something is happening in this town."

Later, he pulled his cruiser into the driveway as dusk fell. Tom heard a scratching behind his trash cans again. "Trash pandas!" he called into the bushes, and then walked in to find Maddie curled up with a book in her favorite yoga gear. "Doctor, what's the most humane way to eliminate raccoons that will also put the fear into their various offspring and familial relations?"

"Don't you dare hurt those poor creatures, Officer Wachowski," Maddie said with a smile. She held up an envelope from her perch on the couch. "Besides, you've got bigger fish to fry."

"No way, is that . . . ?" Tom rushed to snatch the envelope out of her hand.

"Unless someone from San Francisco is

hitting you up for money, it looks like it."

Tom hesitated. "It's small. Is that bad? Should it be bigger?"

"There goes doubting Tom again," Maddie said as she rolled her eyes. "You're worse than me when I applied to vet school. Just open it!"

Tom slowly opened the envelope, then read the letter aloud:

WE HAVE REVIEWED YOUR APPLICATION TO THE SAN FRANCISCO POLICE DEPARTMENT AND PENDING INTRA-DEPARTMENTAL REVIEW AND BACKGROUND CHECK . . .

Tom squeezed the paper in his hand.

WE ARE HAPPY TO INFORM YOU . . .

"I got it!" he yelled.

They kissed and danced around the kitchen. Maddie brought out a cake she had baked him (and tossed the backup one for in case he didn't get it). But she never really doubted him. Maddie always backed Tom 100 percent. She announced her plans to fly out immediately to start scoping out places to live in America's toughest real estate market. Tom felt a thrill at the idea of leaving, but also the sting of his nerves.

Later, after she had gone to bed, Tom snuck out to the garage and stared at his "vision board"—a massive picture of San Francisco's Transamerica Pyramid building shining over the city.

"That's where the action is," he said to himself. "Far away from Green Hi—"

Smash!

Tom ran toward the door with hopes of nabbing a raccoon, but all he could see was the lid from his overturned trash can rolling away in the distance.

CHAPTER 3

It was a rush. A thrill. A rocket ride to the other side and back again. Even if it only lasted for a second.

Sonic could get close to these people. He saw how they lived. He heard what they said. And sometimes, for just a second, he reached out and took a part of their world with him. Then, with a screech of his feet, he was gone. And no one ever saw. That's how fast he was.

"Another day, another flawless run," he

told himself while trying to get a better grip on the day's haul. "Way past cool."

He roared up through the hills and hit the entrance to the cave at top speed. Bouncing around the room, Sonic started to feel a charge shiver up his blue quills, and the heat of his red sneakers as they skipped across the stalactites. Even with the electric trails his oversize hedgehog body traced when he went full blast, he'd never been caught.

"Gotta find a new challenge to keep the old feet sharp, Sonic," he said to himself. Being undefeated was getting boring. Occasionally, he thought it'd be good to be noticed, to talk to someone again. But that was impossible. Years ago, Sonic made a promise to never be seen by a human. But that didn't mean he couldn't push that promise to the very edge.

The hedgehog skidded to a stop and unloaded a few bags of chips, a pair of black sunglasses, and a handful of change onto a crooked shelf with the rest of his collection. It joined his stack of near-mint-condition *Speed Demon* comics, the lone Ping-Pong paddle he used to win the All-Time Hedgehog Versus Self Championship, and, of course, his old-school boom box.

Sonic cranked his favorite song—a lightning-quick beat accompanied by wailing guitars. He kicked and screamed and danced across the rest of his makeshift home. The music echoed off posters of all the places he wanted to run to but could never risk going to. Sonic wished he could shove it in gravity's face by running up the Eiffel Tower. He wanted to ricochet off the pyramids of Egypt like a pinball or dash the length of China's Great Wall in a heartbeat. He had to settle for solo jams in the caves of Green Hills. At least they had good chili dogs here.

Sonic struck the big note on his air guitar and slid into a dresser. Up on top, a gnarled old sack shook loose and landed on Sonic's head. "Ouch!" He gripped his head and squeezed his eyes shut. And when Sonic opened them, he stared at what had spilled out of the sack.

The rings. Longclaw's last rings.

He almost never took them out anymore. He'd been here on Earth so long now, the thought of warping to a stinky mushroom planet seemed insane. He was lonely here, sure, but he was hardly alone. At least there were still people all around him whose lives were like a movie he could control. Sonic was a living fast-forward button.

Take old Crazy Carl, prowling his property every night and snapping bear traps open to catch the alien life-form he knew was just out of reach. That guy was a riot!

Whooosh! Sonic would blow like a gust of wind behind him, and set off every trap in sight. *Ka-Shink! Ka-Shink!* They'd snap off like popcorn.

"I know you're here!" Carl would howl and stomp around wildly. "I know you're real!"

"No, I'm not!" Sonic would call back as he blasted into the hillside. Such good times they had.

But no one kept Sonic's attention like Donut Lord—Green Hills' one-man action force. The affable, pastry-eating do-gooder was the best of what the town had to offer. Dedicated to justice. Friendly with everyone.

Ready for anything. And then there was his animal-loving, yoga-expert wife. Sonic called her Pretzel Lady because of how she could bend, but she seemed like the kind of person just flexible enough to see he wasn't a danger. The kind of person Longclaw had never guessed could live on earth.

Sonic almost felt bad whenever he'd zip through their lives at superspeed, leaving only a trail of weirdness behind him.

CHAPTER 4

"Why do I do it, Doc? I don't know," said Sonic. "Why does the sun shine? Why are the keys of a keyboard not in alphabetical order? Why do they put those little bags of buttons in new pants when they know you're going to throw them out?"

"Een-teresting . . . and you have never considered zat zese 'jokes' are merely distractions from zee real issues you are dealing with?"

"Of course they are," Sonic said while checking out his legs on the psychiatrist's couch. "I mean, I don't even wear pants." He turned his face serious for just a moment and continued.

"Donut Lord . . . he's a man of action, just like me. Any time my speeding around town causes trouble, he always finds a way to keep the peace. He helps me stay out of the spotlight, even when he doesn't realize he's doing it. Donut Lord is basically my wingman. But he's more than that, too. He's . . . he's my best friend."

It sounded silly to say it out loud at long last, but it still felt right. "You can have friends, even if, well . . . even if they technically don't know you exist. That's not so weird. Right, Doc?"

In a flash, Sonic spun around the small

couch and materialized in the psychiatrist's chair, complete with a pair of heavy spectacles and a paper goatee glued to his face. This was a totally normal activity he did and not at all the result of his extreme solitude. "It eez not so abnormal, zat is so," Doctor Sonic said with a raised eyebrow. "But considering your erratic actions of late, do you fear zat your prolonged isolation is making you a bit crazy?"

Whoosh! He was himself again and sitting up on the couch. "Crazy? Me? No way, Doc, you got me all wrong! And on an unrelated note . . . wow, look at the time. Gotta go catch the big game!" He jumped up.

Sonic tore out of the window, leaving behind only a swirl of papers, and he hit the streets of Green Hills as evening fell. He couldn't shake the worry he'd had since he saw Donut Lord and his wife celebrating moving out of town.

With his fur itching for action, the hedgehog skidded into a hiding spot outside the Green Hills junior high baseball diamond. The summer's last traces of a little league showdown was a perfect distraction. At least for a little while. When the game wrapped, winners high-fived in the parking lot, and losers made plans to drown their sorrows at the ice-cream parlor. By the time the people had fully split, Sonic took to the diamond and swung a forgotten bat around with one arm.

If talking to one superspeed version of himself wasn't enough to clear his mind, maybe taking on nine Sonics would do the trick.

He dug his heels into the batter's box and called the play-by-play. "Bottom of the ninth, tie score. And exactly who you want at the plate with the game on the line: Sonic."

Zip! He kicked up a cloud of dirt, ascending the pitcher's mound in a blink. "But staring him down from the pitcher's mound is the most fearsome southpaw in Green Hills: also Sonic."

Swoosh! He tore out to the box of the third-base coach and called out encouragement. "Focus, Sonic. If you win this game, you'll be the most beloved kid in Green Hills! Hit it to the guy in left. He's a real space case." *Zang!* Out to left field, where he stared into the sky and picked his nose.

"Ugh. I can't even with that guy." Pitcher Sonic sneered and wound up for the pitch.

With an arm faster than lightning, Sonic sent a crackle of speed energy out of his fingertips and then raced it to home plate, where he picked up the bat and swung . . .

Cracka-thoooooom!

The blur of a bat connected with his pitch and sent shockwaves across the field. "Yes, yes, yes!! I did it! YES!! Did you see that?!?" Sonic cheered as he sped around the bases in two blinks of an eye. But as he dove headlong into home plate, the ripples of motion faded away, and there was no one to cheer with him.

"Alone," he said at last. "I really am alone . . . forever."

Sonic couldn't stand it anymore. He ran with nowhere to go and found himself rounding first. In an instant, he hit home plate again and started all over. With each lap around the diamond, his red sneakers chopped deeper into the dirt. He made a lap in a blink. Then in a heartbeat. Then in the moment between seconds. And the faster he went, the more his fur and quills tingled with that chaotic blue energy. Faster . . . the air wavered in the heat . . . faster . . . streaks of electric light formed a diamond-shaped vortex . . . faster . . . the world became a blur of hot white lines and then . . .

KA-BOOOOM!

The entire field exploded, knocking even Sonic off course and into the dirt. He squinted and just caught a massive wave of blue chaos energy shooting up and out across the sky. And then everything went dark.

"I never went that fast before," he said in disbelief. "This is . . . not good."

The hedgehog spun through town, finding pitch-black houses and dark streetlights everywhere. The shock of his outburst must have burned out the electrical grid for all of Green Hills. Sonic slowed up around Donut Lord's house. It was as dark as everywhere else in town, but he could hear his friend's voice from inside.

"I know, I know. Everyone in town has called," the Donut Lord said loudly and clearly into his phone as he stumbled outside to his cruiser. "Call Gill to see if he's located the downed line. We'll find out what happened one way or another."

The man stopped and reached into his pocket. He pulled out a long blue quill— Sonic's quill—and his eyes opened wide as it glowed with blue energy.

So that was that. Sonic had finally stepped over the line, and now the humans would be coming for him. His mind raced to the bag of golden rings back at his cave. Would he have to finally take Longclaw's advice? Was it time to warp to another world and leave Green Hills behind?

"No. No way," he said. "It won't come to that. I mean, even after all this, what human could possibly track me down?"

CHAPTER 5

Robotnik knew the odds of an event like that. He'd charted every possibility, run every statistic, crunched every number. He knew this was almost impossible. He was Robotnik. Knowing everything was his job. Now if only those pinheads at the Pentagon would stand aside and let him do it.

His mobile lab rumbled as he pulled off the highway and onto the grassy outfield near ground zero. Robotnik had been contacted twelve hours after the incident. Twelve hours since an electrical shockwave exploded out of Podunk Hills and caused chaos for over eight hundred miles. The defense grid collapsed for fifteen minutes. Electrical shortages reached from St. Louis to the Colorado Rockies. Four satellites in low-Earth orbit burned out. And then twelve hours later, they finally called him in. The fools!

Robotnik stepped out of the armored vehicle and adjusted his horn-rimmed glasses in the midday sun. His mustache shone above his lip, not one hair out of place, and his red lab coat fluttered dramatically. He looked like a superior specimen by any classification. Now to show the yokels that he was.

"Who's in charge here?" he barked as he strode across the baseball field with Agent Stone a step behind.

"That's me. I'm Major Benningto—"

"Nope. Wrong. I'm in charge," Robotnik said, lifting a finger to the stubby-looking military man. "This is a Class Five stellar electrical incident—a coding reserved for only the most unexplained phenomenon. And when a Class Five event is registered, they don't turn over command to G.I. Jerk. They call in someone with the brainpower to operate more than a pop gun."

"And that would be you, Mister—?"

Robotnik snapped his fingers. He was done with this half-wit. Agent Stone stepped up to complete the crude work of speaking to lesser minds.

"DOCTOR Robotnik is the Defense Department's top engagement analyst," Stone said in a clipped tone so beautiful it was almost mechanical. "He has five PhDs, an IQ you couldn't count to, and control over drone technology so revolutionary, your grunts won't touch it for ten years. In a crisis incident such as this, all chains of command bend to his jurisdiction. In short, Major, you're basic. Stand aside."

Robotnik surveyed the baseball diamond as a quartet of lackeys rolled his control board to his side. There was a deep rut dug around the baselines, and no sign that the explosion came from a single source. Intriguing. Somehow, little Podunk Hills contained something that his past jobs (inciting rebellions in foreign countries and spying on every computer on planet Earth) did not— there was a real challenge here.

"Agent Stone, I'm initiating a sweep sequence. Ten miles in every direction should suffice."

Robotnik hacked away on his keyboards with reckless abandon, and his drones hummed to life. The whirring of their blades calmed his nerves and brought a crooked smile to his face. Machines were not like his buffoonish handlers in Washington. They did as they were told with precision and efficiency. And they didn't smell like sacks of sweaty meat.

"Yes, scour every inch, my little botniks," he said as miles of data scrolled across his glasses. "Leave no stone unturned. Ferret out our sticky-fingered attacker so he can be punished like a sick little monkey."

The drones tore through the sky and dove deep into the foliage of the surrounding forest. Their infrared scanners swept across rocks, leaves, and brambles. In minutes, they'd gone miles from ground zero and swung back again, with *beeps* and *bloorps* transmitting every detail back to Robotnik's wild eyes.

And then, in an instant, the needle jumped out of the haystack and poked him in the nose.

"Agent Stone, do you see anything useful in this image?" Robotnik said, zooming in on a section of dirt no bigger than a square foot.

"Nothing at all, sir."

"Of course you don't. You're only human." Even his deadpan yes-man could not compete with the beauty of his botniks.

Robotnik zoomed in on the faint outline of a footprint at the heart of the image and began twisting and warping it with his control board. In moments, a 3-D image of a shoe was before him, and with a dramatic swipe of his hands, the shoe split apart to reveal a tiny paw—more complex than a forest creature's mark, with large flat pads perfect for running.

"Is that what I think it is?" asked the Major, again revealing the depths of his ignorance.

"It's nothing that you could imagine," Robotnik said. "I have determined the precise height, weight, and spine curvature of the creature that left this track . . . but my computer can't find a single match for it anywhere in Earth's animal kingdom. This power outage was no terrorist attack. This is something else. But worry not, my little dunces. Robotnik can track the source of this unclassified miscreant."

Robotnik pressed the controls hard, and his drones rose in formation above his head and shot off into the distance, toward a small cave on the outskirts of town.

CHAPTER 6

Tom took the first calm moment he had since the blackout hit last night and used it to plan his escape. Across his kitchen counter, he spread a large map of the western United States with a thick star drawn around San Francisco in red marker. It went well with the poster of the city skyline Maddie had hung in the garage. All he had to do was figure out the quickest highway route, and he'd be on his way to her.

"It was crazy, honey," he said into the phone as he scanned the map. "The whole town went dark. It was like a sign telling me to get out of Dodge."

"Far be it for me to get in the universe's way, but I don't want you driving out here after a night running around Green Hills making sure no one was hurt," came Maddie's voice on the line.

"Nah, I wasn't out that late," he said. "Besides, they mostly wanted me to save the food from spoiling in their fridges."

"I'm serious, Tom. You can wait to find a cheap flight in a few days."

"It'll be fine. I'll take my time," he said and traced a path in red. "It'll only take me two days. Just me and the open road and not one thought for Green Hills or its paranoid theories or its . . ."

Whump!

"Raccoons!" Tom's eyes lit up as the noise from the garage settled. "They may have made it inside, but they're in for a surprise." He reached into his duffel bag and pulled out a black tranquilizer gun on loan from the department.

"Tom Wachowski, your surprise better not be one of those industrial tranq darts," Maddie said, reading his mind. "Those animals are just hungry. Also, those darts are for bears."

"Of course not. This is just a scare tactic. Love-you-honey, bye!" Tom cut the call off with a swipe of his thumb as Maddie protested. But he knew what he was doing. He just had to shoo the critters off. Perhaps with a warning shot.

Tom crept toward the garage as if he were about to kick the door down to some kind of underworld hideout. That's the kind of thing he'd be doing all day in San Francisco, he was sure. "These raccoons put my partner in the hospital," he narrated like one of his favorite movies. "But they can't escape justice forever."

As he pulled the door open slowly, a few more boxes slid off a high shelf, and Tom heard another sound—a tiny voice. Did these things somehow turn on the radio?

"Just think of a place. Throw the ring. Think of a place. Throw the ring," the high-pitched voice repeated. "Come on, remember what Longclaw said . . . If they find you, go to the next planet. Even if it is boring, and smells weird, and your only companions will be mushrooms of some kind."

Tom spun around the corner and leveled the tranquilizer gun on a pile of fallen boxes just below his San Francisco poster. "SFPD pending background check," he cried out. "Paws in the air where I can—"

And then the electric blue hedgehog looked up at him. It raised its hands— it had hands! It tried to look innocent. "Uh . . . meow?"

"AHHHHHHH!" Tom screamed and the creature yelled back in kind. Before he knew it, his trigger finger snapped and a dart shot straight into the animal's neck. It stumbled, its eyes both surprised and suddenly glassy, and it tossed a large golden ring into the air. That's when things got crazy.

The ring hung in midair in Tom's garage, a faint glow rising to an array of sparkles. Through the middle of the ring, Tom could see his poster of the San Francisco skyline with the Transamerica building dead center.

Then, all of a sudden, it wasn't just a picture; it was more like a window into the height of that tower. Tom reached out his hand to touch the rooftop when the hedgehog finally tipped over and passed out. The ring dropped to the ground. In a second, a brown bag dropped from the animal's paw and slid into the golden window created by the ring.

ZAM!

Tom blinked and the ring was gone. Its vision of the Transamerica building faded, and all that was left was an overgrown, talking forest creature. A blue one at that.

"The Blue Devil," he said, shaking his head. "I owe Crazy Carl an apology . . . I guess."

He carried the hedgehog into the house and laid it on the couch. While he slept, Tom took out the quill he'd been carrying around all day and slid it into Sonic's spiky scalp. A perfect fit. Tom wasn't sure if this made him feel safer or twice as crazy as he'd ever been.

After a while, the hedgehog's heavy breathing lightened, and with a flutter of its eyes, it snapped awake. "Donut Lord?" it said slowly.

"It's real. It's really real," Tom said. "What are you? Why were you hiding in my garage? Are you . . . are you here to abduct me?"

"What?" said the hedgehog, standing up. "You abducted me!"

"Okay, that's a fair point."

"And I'm here because I needed somewhere safe. They came to my home. The last thing I saw was them tearing through my stuff." The animal's eyes grew as it remembered. "And you . . . you're the only person I could think of to turn to, Donut Lord."

"Why do you keep calling me Donut Lord?!"

"Because I've seen you talk to donuts . . . and then eat them if they get out of line."

"Again, fair."

"Wait! Where are all the mushrooms? Why am I still on Earth? What happened to . . . ?" The creature started panicking. "My rings! I lost my rings!"

"Wait, that glowing thing?" Tom asked. "Was that like your mothership?! Because I think it just flew off to San Francisco."

The hedgehog stumbled around and fell back to the couch, still groggy from the tranq. "They're coming for me! You have to help me, Donut Lord! My legs don't work! And my rings are gone. Please! It's life or death!"

That clinched it. Tom had been waiting to hear the phrase "life or death" his entire life. This was it. A real shot to take action as a cop.

Plus, what would Maddie say about a talking animal pleading for its life?

"Okay," Tom said with his sternest action-hero expression. "Come with me if you want to live."

CHAPTER 7

The only thing between Robotnik and
a perfectly automated world was the US
Constitution. If he could shred the blasted
thing in the name of order, he would. But as
it stood, he legally couldn't stride into any
private domicile in search of the creature.
So he had to outthink this simple country
policeman.

"Can I help you?" answered the cop. He
looked like a rube.

Robotnik forced a smile. "Good morning. I'm from the power company, investigating the blackout. If you don't mind, I'd like to take some readings inside your house. Now."

"No kidding, you're from the power company?" The hick stated the obvious. "You must know my buddy Spencer. We play softball together."

"Yes," he replied. "Good man, that Spencer. Now if you'll just . . ."

"Except . . . doesn't the power company usually take their readings outside the house?" the man leaned into Robotnik's face. "Also, my buddy Spencer works for the gas company and he's more of an ultimate frisbee guy. So you wanna tell me why you think I'm dumb enough to just let you inside my house?"

Robotnik ground his teeth. "I'm sorry, Mister . . . ?"

"Wachowski. But everyone calls me Tom. Except my dentist. He calls me Tim and it's gone on so long, it would be weird to correct him now."

"Well, Mr. Wachowski, let's just say I'm authorized to inquire about certain power surges coming from your attic."

"The attic?" the yokel said. "Nothing up there but grandma's hope chest, and you do not want to see what's in there."

He was lying. Robotnik's heat-seeking drone hovered just above the west side of the house, and it was sending all relevant data on an odd infrared mammal to his smart glasses. The creature was in this house.

"Let me explain some facts to you, Wachowski," the mask of kindness dropped from his face. "Fact: About twenty minutes ago we clocked an energy pulse with a similar signature to the one that caused the power outage, and the only house inside the radius of that pulse is . . . 55 Plymouth Road. Fact: I am authorized by law to pursue this as I see fit."

"Fact: You need a mint and a lesson on manners," Tom said. "Listen, Mister . . . ?"

"*Doctor.* Doctor Robotnik."

"Ok, Dr. Robot . . . man," Wachowski said with a sneer. "I'm sure whatever you're here for is very serious, but I have nothing to do with it. Ask anybody in this town. Everyone knows me."

Robotnik's drone slid into the house through an upstairs window. Forget the law. He was going to get this thing. The drone's tiny camera zoomed in on a pile of old sporting equipment. *Blip!* The screen glitched once, and the heat signature—the creature—was gone!

"I bet they do all know you," Robotnik said. "I'm sure you're very popular with all the Jeds, and Merles, and Billy Bobs of this Podunk town. You go way back to the days of playing stickball in the streets or whatever stimulates the dimwits here. And maybe someday you'll achieve your life's goal of getting a Costco card or adopting a labradoodle."

His secondary botnik drone picked up the signature a floor below, not darting but creeping out. He wouldn't lose it!

Robotnik continued to rant. "But the reality is, I surpassed your entire life's achievements before I was a toddler. And I can predict every monosyllabic thought struggling to escape your simple mind before it comes tumbling out of your mouth. So if you think for one minute that you can manipulate or lie to me, Mr. Wachowski, you're even dumber than I already know you are."

His third, hyperfast botnik swung above him. The three drones triangulated. The creature had stopped in the kitchen, cowering.

"Mr. Wachowski, are you familiar with US Code 904, Title 10, Article 104?"

"Of course. It's one of my favorites."

"Anyone who attempts to aid an enemy to the United States shall suffer a potential punishment up to execution," Robotnik said, grinning triumphantly. "And that's what happens if any other government agent catches you. What happens if I catch you will be much, much worse . . . NOW!"

At his command, all three drones smashed through the windows and headed for the kitchen. Robotnik pushed past Wachowski and tightened his fists. He turned the corner to the kitchen and found . . .

An incredibly fat raccoon, gorging himself on leftover cake across a map of California.

"This can't be right," the doctor said with certainty. "I'm Robotnik. I'm never wrong."

"First time for everything," an agitated Wachowski said, stepping in between him and the counter. "If you want, you can take some of this cake to go."

And then he saw it. A pale blue light shone from the counter. Robotnik grabbed and lifted up a long animal quill, glowing with a strange power. It was so erratic, the light of that spike. Chaos unlike his mechanical world, but still powerfully attractive.

"Oh look, I was right. Note my lack of surprise," Robotnik said as he clicked his control pad and the drones spun around their heads. "Five seconds before I let them tear this place apart . . ."

"Listen, pal. I'm the closest thing to the law in this town, so—"

"Five . . . four . . . three . . . two . . ."

"Stop!" a high-pitched voice called out. In the window, Robotnik saw the creature. Close to Earth's taxonomically named Erinaceomorpha Erinaceinae. A common hedgehog. But blue. And speaking. Intelligent alien life was here.

"Don't hurt anyone, dingus. It's me you want," said the creature.

And then, before Robotnik could smash down his control pad, Wachowski punched the doctor square between the eyes. "You caveman!" the doctor cried before the world went black.

CHAPTER 8

"One punch!" Sonic laughed. "You laid him out with one punch!"

Rattatat-rattatat!

From around the corner, one of Robotnik's drones began flashing red and blasting the walls with machine-gun fire. Must have been some kind of self-defense protocol, but Sonic could only shout, "This feels excessive!" as he was yanked from the floor.

"Stay behind me!" Donut Lord said,

and dragged Sonic behind a couch. Sonic's hyperfast metabolism did quick work on whatever was in that dart, but he still could only juice his speed for short bursts. It was now or never to try, though.

"Can you believe Amazon is going to deliver packages with this thing?" Sonic called out as he collided with the drone and grabbed on to its shell like he was riding a mechanical bull. In a second, the whirring robot killer had spun him around and launched him across the room.

His human friend yanked Sonic from the air and sprinted them both out to the lawn. "Oh, don't tell me that's all you got? I'm just getting started. Let me know if you wannna go Round 2 with the Blue!" the hedgehog shouted, and tried not to puke.

Sonic still felt woozy as he climbed into

the cab of Donut Lord's truck. No wait. It was Tom. His real name was Tom Wachowski. *Forget that*, he thought. *This guy is Donut Lord for life.*

"Okay, I want answers, pal. Who are you? WHAT are you?" Tom said as he steered the truck down the side street away from his house. Behind them a bunch of siren-wailing SUVs swarmed the house's front lawn.

"I'm a hedgehog. I feel like that's obvious," he said. "My name is Sonic, and I'm in big trouble."

"Oh, you're in big trouble?! You're not the one who punched some sort of government weirdo back there!"

"You think *you* have problems? I was just trying to live alone, honest," Sonic said. "But something happened, and my powers caused the blackout."

"Whoa, are you, like, on a countdown to explode?"

"No, dude. I'm just a teenager, and everything in my life sucks right now."

"Well, I been there," said Donut Lord sympathetically.

"But we can work it out together," Sonic pleaded. "If you help me unscrew my life, I can do the same for yours. We've just got to get my rings back!"

"Yeah, what is up with those things? I only saw a gold ring for a second, and it was insane."

"Rings are how all advanced cultures travel between worlds," Sonic said. "I was two seconds away from getting away from Earth and to a safe planet. But rather than porting to the mushroom planet, when you shot me my mind grabbed onto that weird pyramid building in San Francisco. Now the rings are on top of it."

"Wait, you mean the top of that skyscraper? The Transamerica building?"

"You know where that is?" It was the best news Sonic had heard in forever.

"It's in San Francisco. We're moving there. Well, we're supposed to."

A look of panic overcame the man's face. "Look, this is the worst possible time for me to get myself in trouble, okay? You asked me to save your life and I saved your life. Now please, go find your rings and your mushroom land. Hopefully I'm about to wake up in some hospital room and the doctor is going to tell me that my colonoscopy was a big success. Okay? So goodbye."

He pulled over the truck and thrust open the door at Sonic's side. Speechless, the hedgehog stepped onto the road.

"Okay, Donut Lord. Goodbye."

"Goodbye," he said to Sonic finally. They stared at each other for another moment. "Why aren't you leaving?"

Sonic shrugged. "I don't know where San Francisco is."

It dawned on the driver what Sonic was hinting at. "No," he said. "No way, I've already got enough trouble with the property values on my now very shot-up house. I'm not becoming a fugitive to boot!"

"If you get me to my rings, you won't be a fugitive! You'll be a hero!" Sonic pleaded. "I can disappear and old Ro-Butt-Nik won't have a thing on you. Come on, Donut Lord! You were made for this."

Tom looked at Sonic and smiled. It was the first time anyone had really looked at him since Longclaw passed. "I can't believe I'm crazy—or desperate—enough to try this. Go ahead and get in the truck before I change my mind. But if we're going to stick together, we've got to play it smart. I can drive through some forested back roads until we're out of Green Hills. I can't risk those drones hurting anyone in this town."

"Right on, Donut Lord." Sonic was pumped.

"But to be extra safe, let's see if we can't shake things up by laying low somewhere, okay Sonic? And if I'm going to call you that, you gotta try out Tom for once."

"Way past cool, Tom," Sonic said. "You won't be getting any trouble from me."

"Like the kind of trouble that comes from you spying on us for years?"

"I mean, I wouldn't call it spying," Sonic

said as the truck pulled back onto the road. "We were all just hanging out, only I wasn't invited and no one knew I was there."

They drove westward on back roads with speed limits way too slow for Sonic. The whole concept of speed limits drove him crazy. And Tom was mostly chill. He listened to Sonic's whole story—his life with Longclaw and his non-relationships with people in town. Sonic learned a few things, too, and felt a little bad about razzing old Crazy Carl. It was wild. He never realized how much he missed talking to someone until he couldn't stop sharing.

But Sonic was getting itchy being trapped in that truck's little cab. Tom wouldn't stop at the world's largest rubber-band ball, or the diner with the best pancakes in three states, or this deer that was giving him the stink eye.

They did none of the fun touristy stuff. It was his first and only road trip, after all.

Finally, into the evening, when Tom stopped at a remote filling station for gas and to call Maddie from a supposedly untraceable pay phone, Sonic couldn't take it anymore. He saw the allure of civilization in a bright neon sign that read THE PISTON PIT. It sounded loud and gross and amazing. Before he knew it, Sonic sped over to the roadhouse through a fleet of gnarly motorcycles parked out front.

In minutes, Sonic was at a table in the middle of the commotion of a loud biker bar. He wore a cowboy hat, an oversized flannel shirt, and a pair of sunglasses that he borrowed at hyperspeed from the various parking lot vehicles. He kicked his feet up on the table as Donut Lord barged in after him.

"Hello, fellow human!" Sonic cheered.

"We're going."

"No way! There's so much I've never done in my life. Now that I'm leaving Earth forever . . . I guess I missed my chance. Let me live a little. I want to order buffalo wings! And guac! I'm not sure what that is but I heard someone say it once. Funny word. *Guac*."

The Donut Lord looked at him for a minute with pity and finally cracked a smile. "Well, this looks like a place a man can get a lot of living done in a short period of time. I guess we can spare an hour."

"You won't regret this!" said Sonic.

"I'm sure I will."

CHAPTER 9

Tom regretted it almost instantly. This hedgehog kid, this Sonic, he was from another world. He had less-than-zero attention span, a permanent case of the jitters, and the loudest mouth Tom had ever seen on something so small.

The policeman in Tom spoke with authority about how the little fella wasn't a kid but a grown man with a "very rare bone condition," but the patrons still stared as he walked by. "Couldn't you have at least stolen some pants to go with that outfit?" he asked.

"No can do, my dude," said Sonic. "You have no idea how comfortable fur is on its own. Probably better than the best pair of pajamas you've ever owned times ten."

They dove into the fun of the roadhouse, and frenzy followed Sonic everywhere. Their dart game was like a needle explosion, each projectile landing anywhere but the bull's-eye. Sonic rode the mechanical bull until he got bored and decided to make it a perpetual backflip pad. Even shooting hoops in the basketball toss drew attention when the little blue nut begged to be tossed in after spinning into a ball (though even for Tom that was a little fun).

But things went off the rails when Sonic

line-danced across the whole place and landed
a red sneaker straight up the rear of a three-
hundred-pound biker with crumbs in his
beard from the seafood special.

"Watch where you're walking, you hipster
doofus!" barked the man.

"Well, maybe if Jerkface McLeatherpants
would watch how much space he's taking up,
we wouldn't have a problem!" The hedgehog
puffed up his quills beneath the cowboy hat.

"Look, it's cool," Tom said, trying to ease
the tension. "We were actually just about to
leave. We're on our way to San Francisco."

"Maybe let your little friend here speak
for himself, dude," said the biker, his spittle
spraying on Tom's nose. Before Tom could
wipe the flecks away, a breeze blew past his
leg. Sonic was behind the biker, his hands on
his waistband.

"Why don't I let your pants say what everyone wants you to do—split!" he said. *Shhhhrip!* The little blue hedgehog tore a wedgie up out of the leather pants and over the back of the biker's head. The biker fell to the floor shouting. By the time Sonic was able to stop laughing, a wall of bikers—all filled with rage—had surrounded them.

That's when chaos broke out.

In every direction that Tom looked, he saw something flying toward him. Chairs. Bottles. Fists. Spit. Screams. But no matter how he jerked, ducked, or swung, nothing hit him. Instead, an electric blue whirlwind sprung around the entire room in overlapping, scribbly lines of light.

Whatever Sonic touched, he transformed into something ridiculous. A dude throwing a tray from the kitchen snapped out of focus until all the chili dogs were eaten off the plate and spaghetti hair covered his eyes. Another attacker found both his feet in rolling mop buckets and then wheeled straight into the love-detector machine. Two massively muscled goons came within an inch of Tom, but with dizzying speed they were wrapped in toilet paper like mummies. It was like the craziest Three Stooges movie ever, in superfast-forward.

In the center of the storm, things cleared just long enough for Sonic to zip up behind Tom, his fists curled up like an old-timey boxer. "This is awesome, right?" the little guy called out.

"Ask me again when I know how many teeth I'm walking out of here with."

Sonic shot off to blue-blur status again. He spun into a hyper-bouncing sphere, ricocheted off the ceiling in loops, and bounced to the ground at odd angles. Even as every move looked like a totally random event, the bikers who were still standing parted and made a kind of tunnel of blue speed that pointed Tom right toward the door.

"Wonders never cease," Tom said as he laughed and made a beeline for the parking lot.

He and Sonic burst out together like a pair of Wild West outlaws. They looked at each other and then booked it for the getaway truck. Sonic was already sitting with his feet on the dash when Tom ran up, out of breath.

"Are they close behind me?" he said as he started the engine.

"Not unless they already climbed over the mountain of furniture I piled up on my way out," Sonic said.

"Okay, but from here on out, we're going

straight to San Fran. No more legally dubious pit stops!"

Tom tore down the road and tried to keep in mind that his dream job was on the other end of this trip. He couldn't mess this up.

"Oh, you loved it in there, Donut Lord!"

Maybe Tom did a little. Maybe he'd been looking for an opportunity to go wild after years bottled up in Green Hills. But he couldn't risk everything to be friends with an alien hedgehog. It was something driven home late that night when the fading radio signal announced, "Manhunt underway for a rogue local, said to have stolen government property. The details of the case are highly classified, but Department of Defense officials say a thirty-something man is wreaking havoc in the company of a diminutive accomplice. Be on the lookout."

CHAPTER 10

Sonic stared out the window at the morning sunlight. They'd stopped behind a billboard to grab a few hours of sleep, and now Donut Lord was winding his way toward San Francisco on a path that Sonic deemed too slow, too crooked, too dull.

"Come on, super cop," he said as he made his hand an airplane out the window. "I thought you were leaning toward being the action-adventure type. Floor it."

"Laying low, dude. That Dr. Robotnik guy seems like he has more than a few ways to track us down," Tom said. "Let's hope that the satellites don't have us pegged already and that Maddie got my messages saying my cell phone was dead. 'Course, it's probably lying in the ruins of our kitchen after those drones went to town."

"What do you care if Robotnik torched your place?" Sonic said. "You're leaving Green Hills, anyway. The best place in the world, and you're selling out for some crazy land of glass sky daggers."

"Do you really not know how small Green Hills is?" Tom asked. "Talk about trying to live your life before it's all gone. I can't do that back home."

"It's not small! There are literally hundreds of people! And, like, three times as many chill animals. And one really rude beaver named Lucius."

"Really?"

"No dude, I'm the only one who can talk!" Sonic shook his head. "You're not making any sense. You come from a great town, with great people. And by my count, zero evil warlords are trying to kill everyone and steal their inexplicable speed energies. That's what it's like where I come from, and I can tell you that only a crazy person would want to leave a place like Green Hills. Besides, what could possibly be more important than protecting the people you care about?"

"Oh please, I clean out their gutters. I jump-start their cars in winter. They can call anybody to do that," said Tom.

"Sure," said Sonic. "They can call anybody. But they don't. They call you."

Before Tom could respond, the sound of shattering glass rang out. A grappling hook broke through their back window and buried itself in the dashboard. Sonic spun around to see a spinning egg-shaped drone on the other end.

"Yahtzee!" called a familiar voice from a speaker on the drone. Robotnik. This creep was turning out to be, well, a creep.

"We've got incoming!" Sonic yelled. "I can bust Ro-Butt-Nik's machine no problem. Just drive the car. I'll take care of this. The way you used to take care of Green Hills!"

As soon as Sonic unbuckled, Donut Lord yanked him back down on the seat. "This time, we do it my way," he said, picking up a tire iron from behind the seat. "Here, take the wheel . . . and keep it steady! I put it in cruise control."

Tom climbed out of the back window, breaking out the rest of the jagged glass as he went. He held firmly to the roof as the drone reeled itself close. Tom swung the iron forcefully at the drone's eye, and the machine spun hard to the left, pulling the car with it.

Sonic responded by jerking the steering wheel back and forth. He ignored the breaks. As the truck swerved left and right across the empty country highway, he saw Tom lurch in the rearview mirror.

"Hold steady!" the Donut Lord called. "Who the heck taught you to drive?"

"Nobody!" Sonic said with a laugh. "I have absolutely zero clue what I'm doing!"

With another wild swing, Tom connected with the drone, popping the cable loose as the front of it shattered into sparking pieces.

"Mr. Wachowski, you don't have to be a

genius to know how supremely stupid that was," called Robotnik's now garbled voice.

As the initial drone sputtered out of commission, a fleet of little baby bots buzzed to life. They swarmed all around Tom and into the truck, circling Sonic's head. The hedgehog swatted at them, and the car careened across lanes. The driver's-side mirror exploded as the truck grazed the guardrail.

"I'm taking the captain's chair back," said Tom as he swung into the driver's seat and pushed Sonic aside.

"Good," the hedgehog said, "because I see where the problem is, and I'm going to fix it."

Like a tranq dart, Sonic blasted off the back of the truck. He hit the highway with his legs pumping as fast as he could and spun into a ball of pure velocity. Nearly four hundred yards back, an armored van was chugging along. It had to be Robotnik's mobile lab.

Sonic struck the center of the van's hood as hard as he could, and with a crunch of the fiberglass, it collapsed, and the vehicle spun off-road. "A real bull's-eye at last!" Sonic cried, skidding to a stop to make sure the van stayed down.

"Do you think the egg drone was the last of my botniks, hedgehog?!" yowled a megaphone voice. The top of the van split open and launched a spider-like dune buggy drone onto the road. It spun out its wheels with a screech and was soon at Sonic's doorstep.

"Tech this ugly is more like Badniks!" Sonic shouted, and bolted back to the pickup.

CHAPTER 11

The truck shuddered when Sonic hit the tailgate and climbed into the back. Tom couldn't believe the old pickup had lasted this long, but it was being pushed to its limits. In the mirror, he saw something black quickly get bigger and bigger.

"You make a new friend?" he called to the hedgehog.

"It's over, Donut Lord," Sonic said through the window. "You have to leave me. Maybe if Robotnik tracks just me to San Francisco, maybe even if he gets his hands on me . . . then you and the town will be okay."

"That's crazy!" Tom said. He was touched this little guy would be willing to sacrifice so much for their safety. And maybe he was feeling a little guilty, too. "You don't owe that town anything."

"Somebody has to!" Sonic yelled, and his quills started to crackle with blue energy. "If you leave, who's gonna judge the Blueberry Festival? Or sit in the dunk tank? Who's gonna do all that stuff?"

"Now is not the time to talk about this, pal!"

The dune buggy bot was right behind them now. Tom floored the gas pedal, but the shaking truck just wouldn't move any faster. The mechanical monster behind them sprouted tiny metal arms that clawed at the pavement just inches from their wheels.

"But it's all going to be over soon. And everyone in that town is going to be left alone, like me!" Sonic cried. His whole body was vibrating with uncontrolled energy now, and Tom could see the fear in his eyes as his rage turned to realization. "Oh no, not again—"

"Sonic, don't—!"

It was too late. The hedgehog jumped off the truck and flew three feet through the air to land on the dune buggy. The botnik shuddered as Sonic's hands reached out in front of him and made a thunderous clap. The shockwave of chaotic blue energy radiated out of those fingers with all its fury pointed back from where they'd come from. In a second, the dune buggy smoked and collapsed on the road. Far back, all the little lights on Robotnik's van went dead. But Sonic was flung back by the force of his own attack and landed in the truck bed with a thud.

Miraculously, Tom still had control of the vehicle. He slammed the breaks and as it peeled to a stop, he shivered at the thought that Sonic might be hurt.

"Hey, buddy! Sonic! Friend! Are you okay?" Tom called, leaping into the back of the truck.

The hedgehog rolled over and flashed a weak smile. "Totally cool, Donut Lord," he said. "Just a teenager reacting to how bad life sucks right now."

Tom smiled wide. "Yeah, I been there," he said. "Let's just be happy that your blackout blast only seemed to kill the road behind us. If it went back far enough, then Robotnik won't be able to call out any reinforcements for a hot minute. Let's get ourselves to San Francisco while we can still make it."

"Donut Lord . . . ," Sonic said as he hopped down and made his way into the cab of the truck. "Tom . . . about what I said about you leaving everyone in town alone. I didn't mean . . . it's just hard for me to see you give up what I can't—"

"Forget it," Tom cut in. "Let's talk about it later. There's a bag of rings waiting for us."

CHAPTER 12

Robotnik gritted his teeth and stormed back and forth inside the newly arrived mobile lab. It had been six hours since that blasted hedgehog fried his last series of botniks, and though his drone-enhanced truck dutifully found him despite his total lack of functioning electrical equipment, he'd still lost too much time to the smarmy Green Hills dolt.

A curse on these commoners. These

small-town hicks disgusted him. The local yokels. The moms and pops. They were forcing him to think the impossible. In order to capture that creature, Robotnik would have to do more than outthink them. He'd have to overpower them. All that was left was a sheer display of brute force.

"Doctor, do we have a calculation on their destination yet?" Agent Stone asked, poking his head in Robotnik's high-tech sanctum.

"Their obvious endgame is San Francisco," the doctor hissed in reply. "Beyond that, inconclusive."

"Amazing that the two of them have been able to stay one step ahead of us this whole time," Stone mumbled to himself—a telltale sign of pedestrian thought.

"You know, Stone, I won't miss you when you're gone," Robotnik said with a sneer, and then launched into his manifesto. "Humans are unreliable and stupid. Space hedgehogs are likely more so. I care very little about either of them or their so-called plans. My machines are diligent, relentless. They mean everything to me, and they will not fail me. You, on the other hand, have one last chance not to fail me. Now bring me what I require to get my juices flowing."

The agent ran out, leaving Robotnik alone with the glory of his own mind, the humming of his flawless machines, and the mystery of the quill. In a sealed glass case, the piece of the hedgehog those twits had left behind glowed—the same glow that had lit the inside of Robotnik's battle van when that creature zapped every electric fuse within forty miles. Now it was time to understand what that meant.

Robotnik flipped the switch on his stereo, and a steady drum machine rhythm pulsated out of the speakers. Funky bass licks filled the air, and the doctor went to work wiring every piece of triangulating tech he had to the blue quill. His eyes went wild with anticipation as his screens sprung to life feeding him data, and his feet took flight in sync with the jams.

Dance! Glorious, undulating movement to the preprogrammed robotic soul of the stereo! Sealed in his workshop, Robotnik could finally shut out the disgusting breathing sounds of his fellow humans and be at one with his pelvic thrusts. The more he stared into the chaotic energy of this hedgehog, the more Robotnik became obsessed with the potential of harnessing its disorder. With that kind of power source, he could convert the whole world into a robot revolution.

Above the captured quill, an energy meter revved up its intensity. Green to yellow to red in seconds as every alarm began ringing in time with Robotnik's pure funky breakdown. "Yes!" he cheered as the distinctive energy signature of the hedgehog fed its data into his computer. "Yes! Yes! Fingerprint that blue freak and bring him to Papa!"

Swack! The door to the lab opened up, and the shadow of Agent Stone fell over Robotnik, mid-thrust. He snapped the stereo off in a swift move and composed himself. Stone suspected nothing amiss, he was certain.

"Um . . . chai tea latte with skim milk, extra hot, just the way you like it," the agent said.

"No foam?"

"No foam."

Robotnik sipped his caffeinated comfort and licked his lips. "Ready the prototype, Agent Stone. And get my flight suit. We're back on the trail."

CHAPTER 13

Tom and Sonic rattled into San Francisco in the late afternoon. How they ever made it, the policeman couldn't figure out. But they were just blocks from the place Maddie was staying in. And if he could find a way to explain to her what the heck was going on, he might have a chance at saving the hedgehog and himself in the process.

Tom knocked frantically on the door to the apartment, and when Maddie answered, he hurried in with a blanketed bundle close to his chest.

"Hi-baby-cool-place!" he rushed in with a nervous smile. "Do you carry, like, cat smelling salts with you when you go on trips?"

"Tom? What happened to you? Are you bleeding?"

He felt his forehead and rubbed off the grime of sweat and blood. "Oh that? Yeah, that's either from the broken window or the robot bee things. It's fine. Anyway . . . cat smelling salts? Or, like, smelling salts for something slightly bigger than a cat?"

Maddie furrowed her brow but pulled a tiny bottle from her first-aid kit. "They don't make smelling salts for cats. But I have human smelling salts," she said, and shot her husband a look. "What's it for?"

Tom laid the blanket down and unwrapped Sonic. He had been slowly fading since he shocked Robotnik's setup, and now the hedgehog's breathing was growing more and more shallow. Maddie's eyes widened and then darted back and forth over the animal's frame, immediately shifting into doctor mode.

"He's a hedgehog, or so he says," Tom said, smiling at his wife's take-charge attitude.

"It talks?"

"Almost constantly."

Maddie put a hand to its chest and two fingers on its neck. "Holy—! His pulse is racing!"

"That might be normal for him, actually. But you've got to help him. He isn't usually this sedate. In fact, he never is."

"I don't know his physiology, but he doesn't seem to have any broken bones.

He's just really banged up," she said, and in a matter of minutes, she had cleaned and dressed Sonic's wounds. Maddie took a deep breath to settle herself and then popped the cap of the smelling salts right under the animal's nose.

"*GottagoFAST!*" Sonic shouted as his eyes snapped open, and then he spun around the room. The blue blur ricocheted off the ceiling and the fridge with a clamor, and then came to rest atop a bookshelf. His breathing never slowed. "Donut Lord! Oh, and . . . hello!"

He sidled up next to Maddie's leg, and she jumped just a hair. "It's Pretzel Lady, right? Good dude you got here."

"It's Maddie, buddy. What is it with you and food?" asked Tom. "More importantly, are you okay?"

Sonic bounced on his heels. "Feels like

everything's here, but I'll be in better shape when we have those rings in hand."

"Tom, can I please talk to you?" Maddie said, her eyes never leaving Sonic. "Hedgehog, you stay here. Try to rest."

"Sure thing. I'm great at resting! I rest faster than anybody!" he said, adding, "And it's *Sonic* the Hedgehog!"

Maddie led Tom out of the room. "Okay. First of all, can we take a moment to acknowledge how under control I've been? I didn't freak out, totally calm," she said, and held out her fist. He bumped it gently. "Secondly, WHAT THE HECK IS GOING ON? IS THAT THING AN ALIEN?!?"

"So, you know how Crazy Carl is always going on about the—"

"The Blue Devil! That's him? He's real?" Maddie touched her temple and processed it all. "What's he doing here? What are you doing here?"

"Well, remember how I told you the raccoons were back? I kinda, sorta shot our little blue friend with the tranq gun."

"You did not!"

"It's hard to explain, but it's crazy important that he gets to the Transamerica building, and I promised to take him," Tom said. He took her by the shoulders and looked deep into her eyes. "I'm still unsure of all the details, but we've got a spook on us that's just a shade away from being a looney tune and . . . more than anything, I trust this little guy. I promised I'd get him to safety."

Maddie's eyes raised with concern at her husband, but it only took a moment until she was back in problem-solving mode. "I have about a million questions, but I get it.

This is the job. Helping people is what good policemen do. It's what you're doing." She bit her lip. "Blue alien hedgehogs still count as people, don't they? I think so."

"I don't deserve you, you know that?" Tom said, and then kissed her before they headed out.

Sonic stood in the middle of the room, a toe tapping like a drum roll. "What took you guys so long?" he said. "Let's go climb a building."

The Transamerica building rose up in the heart of San Francisco's financial district. Tom was certain that from its pyramid-shaped top, you could see everything from the Mission District to the Golden Gate Bridge out across the water. But after Sonic sprinted up the side of the skyscraper at top speed, the hedgehog said the one thing that was out of reach was his bag of rings. The prize had warped on a section of roof fenced off from the ledge, so the only way to get to it was by going inside.

"It's surprising how much people will get out of your way when you flash a badge . . . even an out-of-state one," Tom said as the elevator beeped through dozens of floors. "How long do you think before they call in my future coworkers?"

"Let's hope it's long enough," said Maddie.

"Don't worry. I'll get him where he needs to go and then SFPD can background check me to their hearts' content because he'll be back to being a figment of Crazy Carl's imagination."

"Hey, this figment can hear you, ya know!" Sonic called from inside the duffle bag.

A woman next to them turned in horror. "Do you have your CHILD in that bag?"

"No," said Tom. "I mean, yes it's a child, but no it's not mine." The woman fled at the next floor.

They got off on the top floor and climbed the stairwell to the roof access. Sonic gagged his way out of the bag dramatically. "It smells like Right Guard and old ham sandwich in there," he said, coughing. "What do you do to your body, man?"

"Listen, pal." Tom stopped the hedgehog at the door. "Are you sure you're ready for this? Back on the highway . . . what was with that crazy lightning display?"

"I don't know . . . it's only happened one other time . . . at the baseball field."

"The blackout. What were you doing then?"

"Just playing baseball," Sonic said. He hesitated, then added, "Okay, there might have been some light crying involved."

Tom smiled. "Emotions are powerful things, Sonic. Humans struggle with them all the time. But you don't have to struggle alone. You don't have to bottle it all up."

"Donut Lord, you don't know what it's like when I let that chaos out of me," he said. "I've never seen humans shoot lightning out of their butts."

"Yeah, me neither," Tom said with a laugh. "But wherever you go or whatever you do, you're not just meant for breaking stuff. Leaving Earth, leaving Green Hills behind. That's not you ending something. You can build something good from it, too." Tom didn't want to send Sonic off with the little guy feeling bad about himself. He was going to be a better cop and a better person for having called this troublemaker his friend—and he told Sonic that.

"Thanks, Tom," said the hedgehog. "And thanks for saving my life." They hugged, and then Tom opened the door to the roof.

The rings shone bright in the sun, and as Sonic walked toward them, he began to shimmer with blue energy, too. His nervousness was electric.

Sonic pulled the bag out from its sheltered spot. He held one ring in front of him toward the open sky, focusing hard. Then he turned and said, "Think of where I want to be, and the ring will do the rest." The golden circle in front of him began to glow—

Kra-Boom!

A swarm of drones burst up over the ledge of the building, scattering glass and rubble across the roof. Their high-pitched hum rang in Tom's ears as it was joined by the hum of a rocket. A massive, egg-shaped drone loomed up above them. No, it wasn't a drone. It was a ship of some kind—a sphere of blades and bombs with Robotnik wearing the control harness.

"Don't leave without saying goodbye, hedgehog!" the mad scientist cackled. "Not when I find myself so attracted to you!" The spook was in full supervillain mode, his red jacket fluttering like a vampire's cape.

Tom stepped between Robotnik and Maddie and steeled himself for a fight. "Sonic, I've got things here. You just run!"

"I'm not running away anymore!" Sonic called. Instead, the hedgehog turned and ran straight at Tom and Maddie as hard as he could. "I'm sorry!" he cried.

And then he pushed them over the skyscraper's ledge.

CHAPTER 14

"Well, I was not expecting that," Robotnik said as Tom and Maddie dropped out of sight.

Sonic spun around and faced his tormentor with power crackling across his quills. He only had one chance to make this work. It was a moon shot. A William Tell. A blindfolded bull's-eye attempt in a hailstorm.

And he'd have to do it faster than anything he'd ever tried in his whole life.

"You want to feel the power of the real

chaos so bad?" Sonic taunted. "You'll have to catch me first, Ro-Butt-Nik!"

"Name-calling hurts, you petulant sack of spikes! And challenge accepted!" Robotnik slapped at his controls with fury, and the spinning cloud of mini drones twisted in the air toward Sonic like a slithering tech tentacle.

Sonic launched himself in the air, and suddenly he could see everything in fine detail. He had sensed it at the roadhouse, too, but he was having too much fun then to understand what was happening. All the madness, the mayhem, the pure chaos of the fight slowed down in his mind, and he could perceive every motion of Robotnik's mindless Badniks.

With a light step, Sonic ran up the line of drones and into the air like a kid skipping across rocks in a creek. His sneakers pushed off the bots and sent him spinning right underneath the egg's bulky body. The bag of rings hung loosely in his hand as Sonic spiraled out and ran down the length of the building. He was in some kind of hyperspeed now—traveling at a pace outside the boundaries of reality.

"Aw man, no one's going to be able to hear my jokes now," Sonic said as his feet slapped cracks into the windows of the building. "At least I'm used to talking to myself."

As the cityscape blurred around him, Sonic caught a glimpse of Robotnik's egg-pod flying down the Transamerica building trying to catch him. Fat chance. That thing was a drag. An anchor. A dead weight. But then Sonic caught a glimmer of something in the corner of his eye. It was blue.

Robotnik had pulled up a glass case containing Sonic's lost quill. And with a click, he activated the quill as a chaos power battery. The egg-pod shuttered with a reactive spark, and blue energy started coursing through the entire machine—Robotnik included. Shivers of electricity surged through his mustache, and the creep sped up not quite to Sonic's hyperspeed but close enough.

"Yoo-hooooooooo!" he called to Sonic as the drones caught his pace and came into focus. "Don't run off now, hedgehog! It'll only hurt worse if you do!"

"Don't go too fast, Robotnik! You're bound to hit the wall!" Sonic yelled as he cut back and ran around the corner of the building. He headed for the ground as Robotnik's cloud of metal clashed with the glass, sending shards flying to the street below. Sonic pumped a fist in the air at the sound. He was home free now . . .

Until the egg-pod's missiles blasted off.

Shooooom! Shooooom! Shooooom!

A trio of rocket-propelled explosives curved around the building hot on Sonic's heels. He leaned harder into the run, pockets of glass shattering with each footfall. He could feel the rocket's heat behind him. Sonic needed speed. Crazy, mega, superspeed. He began twisting around and around the building, covering the skyscraper in a net of electric blue lines.

With a zig, he led one missile astray, and it careened into the waters of the bay. Sonic spun around and ran head-on at another. Then, with a jump, he leaped over its nose, tapped a toe on its tail fin, and shot it far into the sky, where it burst like a fiery balloon. The last missile caught up to him at the top of the building, and Sonic led it straight toward Robotnik.

"You think I can't see you?" the doctor cried with wild eyes. "With this power, I can see everything! I'll be able to destroy all that is worthless in this world! Everything will be laid to waste by the botniks, and I will rebuild a flawless world as its god!"

"Speedy delivery for the godhead!" Sonic called, and jumped aside as the missile collided with the cloud of mini drones.

BOOM! The drones shredded to ash across the sky, but the force of the explosion kicked Sonic off his feet. He fell to see Robotnik holding firm in his egg-pod.

"He's got the power of chaos now," Sonic said as he dropped through the air in free fall. "I can't leave him with even a drop of that power." The street below rushed up to Sonic's face, but he grabbed a loose ring and called out. "You want power, Ro-Butt-Nik? You've never seen power like this!"

ZAM!

The ring opened up a portal in the ground, and Sonic fell through, building back up to hyperspeed. The doctor screamed as he flew down after him. "What are those?! What are you hiding from me, you illogical hunk of meat?!"

Sonic tore a path through new ground, and on the other side of the portal stood a sight he'd only ever beheld in the poster on his cave wall: the Eiffel Tower. The ring had delivered them to Paris! Sonic sped through the streets in a haze of blue energy and sampled Paris life as much as he could in the seconds he was there. He inhaled a loaf of French bread to carb up, downed a dozen shots of coffee for a caffeine boost, and slapped a beret on his head for style.

"Ooh là là!" he called, and whipped the hat off to slap Robotnik in the face. The egg-pod was careening wildly, never as fast or as precise as Sonic was when in control of his powers. "Come on, and follow the leader!"

Schwoooooosh! Sonic sped up the side of the Eiffel Tower and left a streak of flames behind him. At its apex, he looked out over the great city and said goodbye. Robotnik rocketed up after him, but before he could reach Sonic—

ZAM!

Another ring warp, and the pair fell onto the top of China's Great Wall. Sonic crouched low and sprinted down the length of the ancient structure. Robotnik swung in the air behind him, but no matter how many missiles the egg-pod shot off, they were all incapacitated by the waves of blue energy spiking off Sonic's body.

Sonic reached into his bag, and he saw that there were only three rings left. "Gotta make it count," he said as he thought of the next place.

ZAM!

A ring warp sent them up into a cloud of thick desert sand, most of it kicked up by Sonic's smoking feet. In the distance, the Pyramids of Giza towered like alien arrows. Sonic spun into a superfast ball, and the lightning he discharged turned sand to chunks of glass as he zoomed toward the tallest Egyptian pyramid.

"There's nowhere you can run from me!" cried Robotnik, his eyes mad with electric power. "I'll destroy everyone and everything in my path to get you, hedgehog!" A final missile launched from Robotnik's egg-pod and bore down on him.

Sonic looked up the length of the pyramid, knowing another second wasted could mean its destruction. "It was a good run while it lasted," he said, and tossed his second-to-last ring in the air.

Zam! Boooooom!

Fire and smoke poured through the other end of the ring portal, and Sonic collided with the ground in the heart of the Green Hills town square. The ring bag bounced off into the gutter. He crawled up on his knees, but the impact of the bomb had shaken him. This was his last chance. His last hope. His final destination. One way or another, it ended here.

"You're an astonishing little creature. It will be fun taking you back to the lab and examining you," Robotnik said as he hovered over him triumphantly. "Any last words?"

"Guac. I like that word."

CHAPTER 15

Zam!

Tom fell flat on his back. Then Maddie
fell flat on him. It was like the drop from
a tree branch times a hundred. "There's no
place like home," he said with a cough.

"Home?" Maddie jumped up and surveyed
Farmer Zimmer's barn. "We're in Green Hills!
How are we here and not dead?"

"Sonic must have tossed one of his
magic rings underneath us as we fell off the

building," Tom said, pulling himself up. "Little dude *is* pretty fast."

"But where is he? How can we help him?"

"I don't know. He may have already warped away, but who knows what happened to Robotnik. All we can do is what Sonic would do . . . keep moving!"

Despite their aches and pains, the pair headed for home at a sprint. Tom burst through the door and surveyed the damage done by Robotnik's drones after his and Sonic's desperate escape. It felt like weeks ago. The room was overturned, books and artwork ripped off the shelves, and Tom's map of San Francisco had been shredded to pieces.

"Someday soon, you're really going to have to tell me what happened to you," Maddie said over his shoulder.

Tom reached down in the mess and

picked up the keys to his police cruiser. "The short version is that robot fandoms can be extremely unhealthy," he said. "But at least we still have a set of wheels to take. Thanks, taxpayers!"

"Where should we go?" Maddie asked. "Back to San Francisco?"

And then, in the distance, they heard the sound of an explosion in Green Hills.

"I've got a feeling we won't need to go that far," Tom said. He nodded to the car. "It might be best if you get in the back."

Tom hopped in and floored it, sirens blazing—the first time he'd ever had an excuse to drive like that as a Green Hills police officer. Within moments, they were approaching a smoldering crater in the town square. Robotnik's egg-pod had come to rest just above the familiar outline of a spiky blue hedgehog.

"Do you trust me?" Tom asked.

"Always," said Maddie.

"Then brace yourself!"

Tom launched the cruiser over a curb and brought it into a head-on collision with the egg-pod. The two vehicles clanged off each other with a *scrunch*, and Robotnik flew from his pilot's seat and onto the ground. The airbag hit Tom square in the face, but he shook it off and checked to find Maddie, unhurt but squeezing the cruiser's cage divider for dear life.

"Now I know what it feels like to be in a cat carrier," she said. "This is professional development, really."

"Stay there and stay safe," Tom said, and jumped out of the crumpled driver's seat toward the action.

"Wachowski!" Robotnik growled as he

pulled himself up. From the wreckage of the egg-pod, strands of blue lightning were still clinging to his warped face. "Who do you think you are, you simpleton?"

"I'm the Donut Lord, chump!" Tom said, and swung his fist hard, connecting with a right hook. The last vestiges of the chaos lightning lifted him off the ground. Tom flipped over and landed in the dirt next to a smiling Sonic.

"I knew you'd make it!" the hedgehog cheered. "Sorry about pushing you off a skyscraper."

"If you had to do it, that was the best way, I guess," Tom said with a laugh.

Robotnik reared up with a snarl and began banging at his busted controls. "Why? Why would you throw your life away for this . . . thing? That's why I only have robots, never friends," he said. "They make you irrational."

Ping!

A D battery bounced hard off of the doctor's head, and Tom turned to see an army of Green Hills citizens, led by Crazy Carl. "That's our sheriff you're messing with!" Carl cried. "And our Blue Devil . . . who everyone can now see is a very real creature who was not at all invented by me."

The townsfolk circled in, but like a rabid animal, Robotnik wouldn't go down without violence. He slammed and swiveled the controls on his glove, and Tom could hear the egg-pod sputtering to life again.

"Do you think you yokels can stop me? ME?!? I am authorized by the United States government to eliminate any and all threats to my investigation, and a much higher power authorizes me to replace each and every one of you with botnik magnificence!"

Zzzzaaaak!

A blue blur crossed Robotnik's face and left him spinning. Sonic the Hedgehog, Tom's friend, was back at full speed and ready to run this creep down.

"You think you got it all figured out, but you played yourself," Sonic said with a jeer as he sped from spot to spot, just ahead of the egg-pod's busted cannons. "You thought you could steal a bit of my chaos energy and use it to bend the world to your will. But it doesn't work like that. Chaos doesn't get controlled, and neither do I, Ro-Butt-Nik!"

"Stop! Saying! That! Name!"

Sonic's quills were charging faster and faster, and his body radiated blue light. Each time Sonic spun around Robotnik, it almost seemed like his body was morphing into a hot, bright yellow flame. Through the blaze of the energy, Tom spotted the X factor for the battle across the field and ran to it.

"Chaos doesn't have to mean destruction," Sonic said, dodging from side to side. "I know how it works now. I know what I'm here for. Introduce a little mayhem into life, and the random ride can bring people closer. That's how you make friends—by sticking together. Right, Donut Lord?"

Tom spun around, the prize in his hand. Sonic had known what he was up to the whole time. The hedgehog could see the big picture after all. Maybe better than he did. "You got it, pal!" Tom called out, and threw the ring sack back toward his friend.

"We'll see how much your friends can offer when I dissect you in my lab!" Robotnik called, though there was fear in his eyes now.

"Yeah, that's gonna be a hard pass from me," Sonic said. "Here's my counteroffer."

The hedgehog caught the bag, pulled out his last ring and sped into an electric tornado. From inside, a golden circle rose in the air, revealing in its center a distant planet populated with mushrooms. Sonic burst out of his whirlwind, supercharged and with eyes like daggers. He clapped his hands together and—

Kracka-THOOOOOM!

A final chaotic burst threw the ring right at Robotnik, eating up the scientist and his cruel machine. A shockwave of blue lightning dissipated in the air, and when the sound of thunder died down, Sonic stood alone in a burned circle of dirt. The hedgehog collapsed.

Tom ran to him, crouching low, and picked Sonic's head up. It didn't look like he was breathing.

"The Blue Devil . . . is he okay?" asked Carl as the townspeople rushed to Tom's side. Maddie was soon kneeling next to him with fear in her eyes.

"He was never a devil, Carl," Tom said at last. "His name was Sonic. And he was always one of us—"

"But I have . . . much better . . . style than you guys." Sonic coughed hard, and his breathing picked up to its regular frantic pace. His eyes fluttered open, and the town of Green Hills cheered.

"That might be," said Tom. "But we still need to get you some pants."

CHAPTER 16

It was a rush. A thrill. A rocket ride to the other side and back again. And it wasn't going anywhere.

Sonic sped through the streets of Green Hills. It was broad daylight, and he could stop anytime he wanted. He spun through the drive-through of the Burger Princess whenever he wanted a free double-decker with cheese. He posted up to Crazy Carl's whenever he needed to borrow something, not a bear trap in sight. He had regular movie nights with a certain young lady (totally casual, mind you).

And most of all, he could pop into his best friend's house whenever he wanted.

It felt strange still, all these weeks later, to be seen. To be known. To be accepted by these people that he had watched from the outside for years. But it was good. He didn't have to hide who he was, and even when his speed got out of control and broke something in town (the local gym had stocked up on treadmill insurance), Sonic was never afraid of driving anyone away.

He swung down the road and pulled up to Tom and Maddie's house, but something was off. A large black SUV sat idling in the driveway. Sonic slowed down and quietly zipped his way into the bushes as a man in black knocked on the door.

"Thomas Wachowski?" asked the stern-faced spook.

"Among other names," Tom said. "Who wants to know?"

"I'm Agent Stone, Department of Defense Special Branch."

"Another one of you guys? I hate to tell you, but we had some trouble with the last one." Tom stepped up defensively. Through the bushes, Sonic squeezed his fists tight in anticipation.

"That's what I'm here about. I've been tasked with cleaning up ops for our division so certain . . . inequities don't repeat themselves," said Agent Stone, handing Tom a package. "Consider this an olive branch for keeping certain matters quiet and a promise that you won't be troubled again."

"I can take a little trouble," Tom said.

"Speaking of which, did you ever find any trail of that Robotnik guy?"

"I'm sorry, no such person exists or has ever existed."

"Oh, how I wish that were true."

"You haven't, by chance, been in contact with a certain alien creature since the incident?" the agent asked. "Uncle Sam would love to have a chat with him. Very casual. A brunch, maybe."

"Who, the Blue Devil? As far as I'm concerned, that's an urban legend."

"Very well, Mr. Wachowski," Stone said. "But keep the package handy, just in case."

Stone's SUV rolled out, and Sonic crept from his hiding place and into Tom's house. He swung through the kitchen and made himself a bag of popcorn, kicking his feet up on the couch.

"What the heck, man?" cried Tom, coming in from the garage. "You don't knock?"

"I thought it was guys' night tonight?" Sonic said.

"It's a little late, pal," Tom said. "Maybe time for you to go back to your cave."

Sonic kicked at the floor and shrugged his shoulders. "Yeah. Cool. I get it. Humans need private time. I'll head out to the hills unless you need me."

"I didn't mean that cave," said Tom. He led Sonic up the stairs to a door that had been locked for weeks. "Figured if I was going to make a go of it in the new, more dynamic, less boring version of Green Hills, I'd need to keep my partner within arm's reach."

Tom opened the door to a bedroom. A real one. The walls were hung with all his posters. An old-school boom box was propped on a desk. And on a shelf along the wall was the last of Longclaw's possessions, somehow salvaged from Robotnik's wrecked mobile lab, and the familiar face of Sergeant Sprinkles.

"Dude!" cried Sonic. "Dude . . . it can't be real!"

"It's real, Sonic," said Tom. "This is home—for both of us. It always has been. I'm just making it official."

"So, no more of the siren call of San Francisco?"

"I think that if we're called to action," said Tom, opening the package from Agent Stone, "It'll come from someplace else." He held out a slick, next-level radio receiver.

Sonic took the device in hand. "Secret government hotline," he said. "Way past cool."

Life moved pretty fast, but finally Sonic

wasn't alone anymore. And who knew, maybe he'd get a chance to make even more friends down the road?

EPILOGUE

Far away, the wind howled over the ocean. Storms wracked the cliffs and the water was rising with the tide. Something big was coming. Something that no one in this world could ever expect.

The wind twisted and turned, picking up leaves and branches in its power. The debris swirled in a small twister, and sparks began to flicker in the air as if by magic.

Zam!

A flash of lightning split the air in two, and soft feet landed on the ground above the cliff.

"If these readings are accurate, he's here," said the fox, as his two tails twitched in the wind. "I just hope I'm not too late."

Worlds away, the heat of the jungle made dew drip off the mushroom pads, and a sharp knife of repurposed metal cut its way through the brush.

"Doctor's log: Day 45. Still marooned," Robotnik recited into the data pad that flickered on his wrist. Behind him, the remainder of his egg-pod lurched as he yanked on its vine reins. "But thanks to my supreme intellect and specially formulated mushroom diet, my grasp on sanity remains absolute."

The doctor paused and tilted his wild hairy head to listen.

"What's that, Agent Stone?" he said to the toadstool that sat on the machine, its front painted with a sticky pair of sunglasses. "Thank you. I like your new look, too."

He pressed on in the heat. Over a month and still no signs of intelligent life on this rock. What bliss. "An uninhabited planet. No supplies. No apparent way home. A lesser man would die here," Robotnik said as he smiled through his mustache. "I'll be home by Christmas."

THE END